PECULIAR PETS

2021

Amazing Poets

Edited By Roseanna Caswell

First published in Great Britain in 2021 by:

![Young Writers Logo] YoungWriters® — Est. 1991 —

Young Writers
Remus House
Coltsfoot Drive
Peterborough
PE2 9BF
Telephone: 01733 890066
Website: www.youngwriters.co.uk

All Rights Reserved
Book Design by Ashley Janson
© Copyright Contributors 2021
Softback ISBN 978-1-80015-585-5

Printed and bound in the UK by BookPrintingUK
Website: www.bookprintinguk.com
YB0474M

FOREWORD

Welcome Reader!

Are you ready to discover weird and wonderful creatures that you'd never even dreamed of?

For Young Writers' latest competition we asked primary school pupils to create a Peculiar Pet of their own invention, and then write a poem about it! They rose to the challenge magnificently and the result is this fantastic collection full of creepy critters and amazing animals!

Here at Young Writers our aim is to encourage creativity in children and to inspire a love of the written word, so it's great to get such an amazing response, with some absolutely fantastic poems. Not only have these young authors created imaginative and inventive animals, they've also crafted wonderful poems to showcase their creations and their writing ability. These poems are brimming with inspiration. The slimiest slitherers, the creepiest crawlers and furriest friends are all brought to life in these pages – you can decide for yourself which ones you'd like as a pet!

I'd like to congratulate all the young authors in this anthology, I hope this inspires them to continue with their creative writing.

★ CONTENTS ★

Castle Douglas Primary School, Jenny's Loaning

Leigha McGarva (10)	1
Callum Bateman	2
Adam Pringle (10)	3
Lexi Low (10)	4
Ria Marshall (10)	5
Ben Williamson (10)	6
Jake McCubbin (10)	7
Keighla Kirkpatrick (11)	8
Saffron Slee (10)	9
Rylan McClements (10)	10
Fraser Cunningham (10)	11
Kelvin McElroy (10)	12
Jazmine Debnam (10)	13
Dylan Jardine (10)	14
Isla McClements (10)	15
Fern Craig (10)	16
Riley Sharpe (10)	17
Tyler Drummond (10)	18

George Watson's College, Edinburgh

Cosmo Bain (10)	19
Sarah Loudon (10)	20
Christian Wong (10)	22
Loriana Radomirovic (10)	24
Sienna Crolla (11)	26
Tara Harrison (10)	28
Hannah Darroch (10)	30
Evie Mae Cattanach (11)	31
Orla McCafferty (10)	32
Alex Southwell (11)	33
Robbie King (10)	34

Charlie Kilpatrick (10)	35
Nia Jenkins (10)	36
Angus Collingboune (11)	37
Sydney Cheyne (10)	38
Helen Willder (11)	39
Rory Burden (11)	40
Robbie Turner (11)	41
Ruby Sharp (10)	42
Joe Henson (10)	43
Evie Dunbar (10)	44

Keith Primary School, Keith

Cameron Simmers (10)	45
Lexi Newlands (10)	46
Connor Milne (10)	47
Evan Wightman (10)	48
Charlotte Milne (9)	49
Dion Moir (9)	50
Leonie Bayliss (10)	51
Jacob Winton (9)	52
Emma George (10)	53
Lewis Simmers (10)	54
Megan Jamieson (9)	55
John Young (9)	56
Ellie-Mai Simpson (9)	57
Kaiden Moir (9)	58
Amy Spence (10)	59
Khianna Mackie (10)	60
Brett Barr (10)	61
Evie Morison (9)	62
Lauren Sinclair (10)	63
Finlay Marwick (9)	64
Olivia Bury (9)	65
Angus Duncan (9)	66
Skye Fraser (10)	67

Ryan McWilliam (10)	68
Edith Malcolm (9)	69
Callum Duncan (9)	70
Meg Malcolm (9)	71
Aiden Rodger (9)	72
Lily Ewan (9)	73

St Gregory's RC Primary School, Ealing

Noora Al-Bazi (11)	74
Julia Cheesman (8)	77
Dominik Kaim (11)	78
David George	80
Rihanna Sriskantharajah (10)	82
Aimee Paget (11)	84
Thomas Jeffs (11)	86
Eva McLoughlin (9)	88
Connor Devlin (11)	89
Kacper Sporek (9)	90
Flossie O'Meara (11)	92
Lucas A (8)	94
Olivia Miller-Noya (11)	96
Dante Kulasingam (10)	97
Sara Iwaniec	98
Edward Jeffs (9)	99
Mykah Perez (9)	100
Philip Strzelczyk (9)	101
Caroline Sideso (11)	102
Myles Pierce (8)	103
Michaela Kesselly-Moore (9)	104
Giuliana Sofia Franklin Tijaro (8)	105
Khloe Francis Nwaka (10)	106
Julia Trzeciak (11)	107
Layla Keenan (11)	108
Hugo Pawlak	109
Giacomo Collins (8)	110
Sebastian Grundy (8)	111
Francesca Studnik (9)	112
Michal Brogowski (10)	113
Melissa Griffin (11)	114
Alexander Owsiany	115
Alan Nerka (10)	116
Patryk Tober (11)	117

Adam Chorebala (11)	118
Ruslana Balabukh (11)	119
Orla Fryatt (10)	120
Mateusz Szarek (11)	121
Olivia Fashade (9)	122
Emma Lukomska (9)	123
Tala Glover (9)	124
Anaiya Rainford-Celestine (11)	125
Amelia Wright (9)	126
Arlo Johnstone (9)	127
Shannon Moynihan (9)	128
Luiza Tarasek (9)	129
Zaria Fa Kusi	130
Vivienne Yassa (8)	131
Aoife Stewart (11)	132
Conor Whyte (11)	133
Estella Thompson Oakley (9)	134
Tymon Urbanowicz (9)	135
Aaliyah Humphries-Brown (8)	136
Lily Hunter (9)	137
Tiphaine Riou (11)	138
Olivia Ryan (9)	139
Adam Holland (11)	140
Elsie May Lettis (9)	141
Patryk Kozlowski (10)	142
Maria Grazia Della Gatta (9)	143
Alan Romanczuk	144
Saiyen Pillay-Gomes (9)	145
Alex Sobiczewski (10)	146
Rita Kozub	147
Tymon Kowalik (9)	148
Excel Etteh (9)	149
Abiana Alexandru (8)	150

Woodlands Primary School, Linwood

Ava Barr (9)	151
Jack Irvine (8)	152
Nathan Kay (9)	153
Isla Hampsay (8)	154
Hannah Madden (8)	155
Jacob Sindhar (9)	156
Kaylah Boyce (9)	157

Laura Reid (8)	158
James Tweedy (8)	159
John Ward (9)	160

THE POEMS

Rocco And Layla

R occo
O nce looked outside, he barked for no reason
C ool times will never end
C ool things are awesome like family is cool
O llie could do weird things after sleeping

L ovely
A nimals
Y ou could never forgive things like this
L ayla liked everything, especially her favourite people
A nd when she bites, it tickles. She falls and barks.

Leigha McGarva (10)
Castle Douglas Primary School, Jenny's Loaning

The Ballistic Bunnies

O reo catches crazy cookie crumbs
R idiculous, random and reckless
E nergetic
O reo is my bunny and I love her

B reathless, bounce and bulky
R idiculous and random
A lphabet all the way
M urmur Marmalade, magnificent
B ramble is my bunny, a very loving one too
L iving in lavender soil too
E lephant in alphabetical order!

Callum Bateman
Castle Douglas Primary School, Jenny's Loaning

Peek-A-Boo's Movie Thing

P icking up food in their little bowl
E ating it quickly, then running so fast
E rrands upon errands until they get tired
K icking back up the very next day
A ll the time, they're so happy, it makes us full of glee
B ouncing around all the time
O ver the hills made of dirt
O ver the hills made of rock, but then they get so tired.

Adam Pringle (10)
Castle Douglas Primary School, Jenny's Loaning

Jasper

J asper jumped over the highest bridge ever
A ll you could see was the sight of a golden retriever
S parkling retriever in the air, flying over
P eople stood there in shock, as Jasper's eyes did glow
E ven shinier than a gem, his eyes glow
R ight after he jumps over the bridge, all you could see was a glowing golden retriever.

Lexi Low (10)
Castle Douglas Primary School, Jenny's Loaning

Coco And Ernie

C razy, if you might not know
O verexcited when she goes for walkies
C oco is a dog, not a cat, silly!
O bviously, she loves her treats

E very winter he hibernates
R eally cute, obviously
N ot a toy, a tortoise
I 'll spoil him lots
E ats lettuce and veggies.

Ria Marshall (10)
Castle Douglas Primary School, Jenny's Loaning

Gweble Gog

G weble Gogs are cool
W e don't find them in the woods
E very Gweble Gog has a different colour
B lue Gweble Gogs eat meat
L ions eat Gweble Gogs
E very Gweble Gog is cool

G ogs are great tree climbers
O r amazing builders
G weble Gogs are amazing eaters.

Ben Williamson (10)
Castle Douglas Primary School, Jenny's Loaning

Buttercup's Day

B uttercup, come on in
U nder the roof
T his is her bed
T iny dandelion
E ats coo cakes
R uined in the rain
C oo cake is so nice for cows
U s, we just don't like it
P eople put it in the bin.

Jake McCubbin (10)
Castle Douglas Primary School, Jenny's Loaning

Marvellous Dogs

M y
U nfashionable
R unning
P artying
H ungry
Y elper

C ute
A nimal
I love the most
L ike a fluffy puppy
L ovely thing
Y ou are an adorable dog.

Keighla Kirkpatrick (11)
Castle Douglas Primary School, Jenny's Loaning

The Amazing Froppy

- **F** un to have when it comes out to play
- **R** apid like a cheetah
- **O** verwhelming like a kitten
- **P** erfect pet, my tiny little frog
- **P** urple stripe down its back
- **Y** ellow circle on its stomach.

Saffron Slee (10)
Castle Douglas Primary School, Jenny's Loaning

Floppy

F loppy is a fantastic dog
L oving Floppy is so nice
O bsessed with eating treats
P etrified of people knocking on the door
P ork is her favourite food
Y ank is what I do on a walk.

Rylan McClements (10)
Castle Douglas Primary School, Jenny's Loaning

About A Labrador

This bear rhyme
If you have time
My pet is a Labrador
"I can't do chores!"
Said the Labrador
I get called a boar
A boar is a pig
I am not wearing a wig
I am a Labrador
Not a boar.

Fraser Cunningham (10)
Castle Douglas Primary School, Jenny's Loaning

My Poem About My Dog, Walter

W eird noise whining
A dorable and agile
L ate
T wo tempers, growling and biting
E ating meat and dog treats
R ight as in knowing we're going on a walk.

Kelvin McElroy (10)
Castle Douglas Primary School, Jenny's Loaning

Bashy

B eautiful sixteen-year-old pup
A dorable dog who loves her mum
S weet and kind, wouldn't even hurt a fly
H appy when goes on walks
Y ummy, yummy treats.

Jazmine Debnam (10)
Castle Douglas Primary School, Jenny's Loaning

Danny, The Dj Dog

D anny is a dramatic dog
A mazing at being a DJ
N ot scared to perform
N ot scared of other dogs totally
"Y ummy," he says when he smells food.

Dylan Jardine (10)
Castle Douglas Primary School, Jenny's Loaning

Bella

B ella, my dog, is fluffy like a sheep
E very day, she meets me at the door
L ovely like an elephant
L icks my face
A fter school.

Isla McClements (10)
Castle Douglas Primary School, Jenny's Loaning

Theo, The Thumping Lamb

T humping around in his blue and purple coat
H aving the best fun
E ven jumping around and running about
O verall, he is the best lamb ever!

Fern Craig (10)
Castle Douglas Primary School, Jenny's Loaning

Gorge The Cat

G ood little cat
O verexcited cat
R eally funny little thing
G entle, little, furry
E xtraordinary cat.

Riley Sharpe (10)
Castle Douglas Primary School, Jenny's Loaning

Marvellous Marvin

Marvellous Marvin is a marvellous cat
Marvin sleeps on a marvellous mat
Is Marvellous Marvin from Mercury?
Maybe I'll ask him one day.

Tyler Drummond (10)
Castle Douglas Primary School, Jenny's Loaning

Dilly The Duck

Dilly the duck is quite silly
And a little bit smelly
And has quite a big belly
He strides along the water
To have a wash
Not knowing he was quite daft
And instead, he was in a bath
He was chilling in the water
Feeling the vibe
When suddenly, a dog arrived
It tried to gobble Dilly up
Dilly got scared and he decided to go up
He flapped his wings with all his might
He flew up into the night sky
He forgot about the roof
He banged his head
And landed with a *sploosh!*
"Bark!" went the dog as he ran away
"Hooray!" said Dilly, as he was safe for today.

Cosmo Bain (10)
George Watson's College, Edinburgh

Toby Gets A Girlfiend!

One day, when Toby was on a walk
He saw a beautiful elephant wearing a frock

Toby was so amazed that he started staring
And she started glaring
Because she was pink
He wasn't looking where he was going
So he stepped into a puddle
And started to sink

Without thinking, the pink elephant ran
As fast as she could and stood
Right on top of Toby's shell
Surprisingly, it made quite a smell

Finally, after about ten minutes
She lifted her bright, heavy foot and said,
"I am a magic elephant, please ask me three wishes."

"Ooh, I've never met a magic elephant before
And by the way, you're looking very pretty today!"

"Please give me your wishes!" said the elephant
"Oh and please call me Ellie."

"I wish that... you could be my girlfriend
And our relationship lasts forever!" shouted Toby

"Okay..."
A huge beam of light sparkled over Toby and Ellie
And they were suddenly holding paws
"Ah, I'm going to love this!" said Toby, loving his life.

Sarah Loudon (10)
George Watson's College, Edinburgh

Alfie, The Albatross

Alfie the albatross had one difference
Amazingly, he looked like an ostrich
He waddled around and squawked all day
Until he finally got a stitch.

All of the other birds laughed at him
But he didn't care a bit
He ignored it all and shrugged it off
And the others all got a fit!

One day, he flew off into the sea
He could fly, what a surprise
And he got lost pretty quick
Which was a little unwise!

He turned back, rather annoyed
And he didn't know what to do
He lay on the floor distraught
He didn't have a clue!

But he found a kind old bird
Who gave him some advice

He went from the cave smiling
With seven teeth, to be precise!

Ever since he's been joyful
And he now has lots of friends,
He feels on top of the world
And it will never end!

Or will it?

Christian Wong (10)
George Watson's College, Edinburgh

Floppy The Party Animal

Every day and every night, I think
And blink and blink and blink
Because it's so hard to believe
It's as hard as the cuff on my sleeve
I won't keep talking on like this
So I'll just tell you what it is

Once, while visiting family
By the way, they have very good taste in tapestry
We were all eating breakfast
When Aunt Moe said we needed to go to the dentist
We all got in the car, but wait
I heard a sound from the house
And it definitely wasn't a mouse
So I walked back into the living room
And *wallop! Bang! Boom!*
There was a dog party going on
But when I got Aunt Moe
They were all gone!
The only dog left was Floppy
And he had confetti in his fur

But Aunt Moe's eyesight was a blur
So the truth won't be known
So don't, don't, don't
Leave your dog alone!

Loriana Radomirovic (10)
George Watson's College, Edinburgh

Superhero Sam

Let me tell you about the story of Sam
The superhero cat
Sam the cat wasn't really a superhero
But his time was about to come

Sam couldn't jump very far
But he knew he would soon be a star

Sam got teased by other cats
Which made him doubt
If he would ever be a star

But one superhero Sunday
It was suddenly Sam's time to shine

Sam the cat looked outside
And found a tragedy with a tree

Sam rushed outside
To see what the commotion was

You wouldn't believe what happened
Next, a cat was stuck up a tree

So, *whoosh!* Superhero Sam
Went outside and saved the cat
And soon Sam was the most
Popular and coolest cat in town!

Sienna Crolla (11)
George Watson's College, Edinburgh

Pennie's Trip To The Seaside

I have a pig called Pennie, she is such a diva
Pennie loves dancing and wanted to be a ballerina

Yesterday, we went to the seaside
Which Pennie begged for
We had to go with Pennie's annoying friend, Meg

First, we got candyfloss
They did not have pink candyfloss
So they started yelling
They are such divas

Next, we went on the Ferris wheel
Pennie and Meg just had to squeal
And yell to slow down
They are such divas

After that, we went on the Jelly Bean
"Why, why, why?" they were gonna scream

Sadly, it was true
Help me, I was so blue

By the end of this, I was sad and blue
Help, I really need a diet Coke.

Tara Harrison (10)
George Watson's College, Edinburgh

Clara, The Clumsy Cat

C ool as a cucumber, Clara crept into the cake shop
L owering her head, she sniffs the floor for food
U sing her senses, she makes her way to the cake aisle
M oving slowly, she snatches a piece in her mouth
S tomping, out of the shop she slips
Y elling loudly, the shopkeeper chased Clara out

C rawling under the gap, back into her garden
L ying on the warm grass
A ching really bad
R eady to dive into her cake
A t last, she finally has a nice meal.

Hannah Darroch (10)
George Watson's College, Edinburgh

Geraldine, The Sassy Giraffe!

Geraldine is a sassy giraffe but she has a very small neck.
At the weekends, she likes to ride on her unicycle,
She gets very dizzy, which makes her hair go very frizzy.

She gets very annoyed at her brother,
But luckily, it's nearly summer!
In the summer, her brother goes to camp, to become a champ.

Gee is very bossy, luckily to calm her down she drinks some coffee.

She always meets her friend, Daisy the dog
Who shares her bows as they have an extraordinary friendship.

Evie Mae Cattanach (11)
George Watson's College, Edinburgh

Penny Penguin

P enny is a penguin, she can fly
E xcitable she can be
N ever afraid to fly up high
N ever afraid to be seen
"Y ou can fly!" she tells the others

P andas are her favourite animal
E xcited around pandas
N ever afraid of flying to see pandas
G enerally not clumsy but sometimes is
"U p, up and away!" you hear her shout
I n the air is her favourite place
N ice to meet you!

Orla McCafferty (10)
George Watson's College, Edinburgh

Sally, The Silly Snake

Sally the silly snake loves to slither and slide
With her friends, Sassy, Syd, Slimy Summer
And Slidy Samantha
Except she has two heads
She knows she's not an ordinary silly snake
But she likes to be silly, sassy
And all the ordinary things snakes do
But she gets teased by Selfish Simon a lot
He is really selfish and sassy
But she slithers away when he is savage

When she slides into her silky house
She slithers into a ball and falls asleep.

Alex Southwell (11)
George Watson's College, Edinburgh

Karate Kitten!

K arate Kitten was not a normal kitten
A t home, Karate Kitten smashed up the house
R idiculously, when a pit bull terrier saw him, with one swish of his mighty, but furry, tail, the dog was knocked out cold
A t the human world Karate championships, ten swishes of the tail, ten opponents defeated
T ea with the Queen, that was his prize, he threw the tea out of the window, that's what Karate Kitten did
E at proper food! thought Karate Kitten.

Robbie King (10)
George Watson's College, Edinburgh

Sapphire, The Smart, Silly Peacock

Sapphire, the smart, silly
But incredible peacock
Likes to fly
You may think
A peacock that flies is stupid
Sapphire likes to play with
Sam, Sofia, Sophie, Skyla
Scott, Sasha and Spencer
Some of his friends like to slither
His favourite day is Sunday
He slices things with his feathers
Sometimes silly, smart Sapphire
Gets bullied by Selfish Sebastian
He is selfish, very selfish
Sapphire likes to fly in the sky
And swim in the sea.

Charlie Kilpatrick (10)
George Watson's College, Edinburgh

Connie The Cat

C onnie is a peculiar cat, she's different to the rest
O n starry nights, she goes outside and admires the stars and moon
N ow no other cats are like this, which means they laugh and mock
"N o other cats are like you!" they say, which makes Connie sad a lot
I n the world, the only one who does this in a way
E nough is enough! she would think to herself, which meant she never failed.

Nia Jenkins (10)
George Watson's College, Edinburgh

Hinky The Hamster

Hinky was a hamster
She had huge cheeks
She could hold anything
Even a peach

One day, she was eating a cherry
The next day, we were
Going on holiday on a ferry

We took her with us
And set onto the boat
Suddenly, Hinky was not there
I looked around
Then I realised I had started to swear

The floor shook and Hinky emerged
And then the boat quickly submerged...

Angus Collingboune (11)
George Watson's College, Edinburgh

Daisy, The Dancing Dog

Daisy the dog loves to dance and wear bows
Daisy has so many clothes
When she gets a party invite
She thinks it's a fashion show
When it's time for her dancing show
She makes her face glow
And if she was not the leader
She would blow a giant fit
So she would perform
Every Sunday, she would meet
Her friend, Geraldine the giraffe
They would share their bows.

Sydney Cheyne (10)
George Watson's College, Edinburgh

The Doughnut Shop Cat

Candy the cat works at a doughnut shop
She never tires and loves what she does
She serves hungry customers non-stop
But watch out if you buy a doughnut
Because Candy loves doughnuts so much
She licks every one that she makes
So every time you buy some doughnuts
Look for the ones that she touched
For every so often, you will find
Teeth marks in the cakes!

Helen Willder (11)
George Watson's College, Edinburgh

John The Bear

J ohn, the grizzly bear, was not a usual bear, he could play the guitar
O h, John was huge and brown with white spots. About three metres tall
H e toured the world with his band, Death Bear, his solos were the best
N ow John is retired, but still rocking with his bear guitar.

Rory Burden (11)
George Watson's College, Edinburgh

Henry, The Long-Tailed Dog

H enry hated his long, long tail
E very day, people stood on it and tripped over it
N ever has there been a day he hasn't had it tangled
R yan, his best friend, liked playing with his
Y o-yo. Henry liked Ryan, but he didn't like his tail.

Robbie Turner (11)
George Watson's College, Edinburgh

Larry The Lizard

L arry is very fast
A ctually faster than Usain Bolt
R eally fast, I couldn't see where he went and I lost him
R ight, I need to find him
Y ou're serious? This is so annoying, I think he might have super speed!

Ruby Sharp (10)
George Watson's College, Edinburgh

Doggy Dug!

My name is Dug
And I'm not normal
I can fly
Pretty cool, right?
I use my tail and these orb things
And I wag my tail to levitate
But to fly, it is quite hard
I have to jump off my special sofa
And wag my tail.

Joe Henson (10)
George Watson's College, Edinburgh

Hally, The Human Dog

Hally is a human dog
Hally likes walking through bogs
Hally loves eating
Hally likes reading
Hally likes old black cats
Hally loves sleeping on new blue mats
Hally lives in a new modern box
Hally has a brown toy ox.

Evie Dunbar (10)
George Watson's College, Edinburgh

Peter Panther

P eter the panther is my very best friend
E verybody thinks he is an extraordinary joke-teller
T he very thing is that he is never around because he is a billionaire
E very bit that the light touches is his and mine
R eally, he's a star, but I wish he was around

P laying is his favourite with me and Tommy, the tiger his other best friend
A vengers: Endgame is his favourite film
N ever telling lies about his work
T he thing is he's the best pet on Earth
H e loves reading Harry Potter books
E xtraordinary is one way to describe him
R eally he's great!

Cameron Simmers (10)
Keith Primary School, Keith

Coco The Bunny

C oco is a bunny, a really funny bunny
O ranges are Coco's favourite fruit
C ute, fuzzy and soft
O f course, it's a pet, it likes to play with a net

T ames itself alone in the woods and it's so good
H as the best sparkles, as sparkly as a star
E ven so, it's a superhero, it can still have fun

B iffer is Coco's best friend
U nicorns are Coco's favourite pet
N obody has this pet, except me
N o animal is as cute as Coco
Y ou know you want Coco for a pet.

Lexi Newlands (10)
Keith Primary School, Keith

Monty The Cat

When I was jogging home from school, I saw
The strangest sight I had ever seen
So strange in fact, I didn't think it was real
A cat carrying a shopping list and holding car keys
I followed this strange cat to its car
As it was climbing into the car, I saw its name
On the collar, it said: 'Monty'
The strange thing was, he owned a Bentley
Continental GT
And an old lady was in the driving seat
When the woman started to drive out of there
The cat opened a book
And that's when I knew I would never see this again!

Connor Milne (10)
Keith Primary School, Keith

Marvellous Max, The Cat

M arvellous Max is a superhero
A lso, he can shoot lasers from his eyes
R oyal and intelligent
V ery tall, to be exact, 35cm tall
E very night, he goes out to look for crimes
L ook out, it's Marvellous Max
L ucky and cool
O verseas to other countries
U seful and perfect
S afe and friendly and saves people

M illionaire and has a mansion
A ctive and playful
X -ray vision to find his enemies.

Evan Wightman (10)
Keith Primary School, Keith

Surprled, The Fox

S urprled, the fox, is a nice and friendly fox
U p to the moon, she loves the moon
R uby is her real name, she likes rubies, but she is a witch
P robably she loves black and green but she is a lovely girl
R uby is an extraordinary witch
L ikes art, school, being a witch and she loves her with hat
E ven more excited when she wears her witch hat
D rizzle cake is lemon cake, it is Surprled's favourite food.

Charlotte Milne (9)
Keith Primary School, Keith

The Pupacorn

    P eaches are Pupacorn's favourite thing to eat
yo **U** can feed it with sweeties and it will turn rainbow
    P upacorn is a pro dancer, she is better than everyone else
    A t its tail is a dog's tail. It is as furry as a bunny
    C ute Pupacorns are when they are babies
    O n its head, there is a sharp horn as sharp as a knife
    R ainbow PupaCorns are the best, they are legendary
    N avigation car that is rainbow.

Dion Moir (9)
Keith Primary School, Keith

Hound

My German Shepherd is one cool hound
He shops and likes to spend a pound
His favourite treat is buying meat
He wears cool trainers on his feet
My German Shepherd's coat is blue
He has a really weird hair-do
His bark is really loud and deep
And he likes to have a sleep
He loves going on walks
But the door is always locked
He thinks that is very bad
So he is very sad
He is a very good pet
But he hates going to the vets.

Leonie Bayliss (10)
Keith Primary School, Keith

Jason The Pig

J ason the pig is one of a kind
A lways eating food from Tesco
S ometimes saving the day with CTP
O n patrol at Tesco and Aldi
N ever being mean to CTP and Tesco and Aldi staff

T elling lies again and again
H ope for his future and other people's
E nding battles safely

P ulling pranks on everyone
I t's the coolest pig ever
G reatest animal on Earth!

Jacob Winton (9)
Keith Primary School, Keith

Sassy Sally

S assy Sally is my sassy duck
A duck as sassy as a teen
S he is as clever as a fly
S he is as fluffy as a pillow
Y ou won't want this sassy hoarder

S assy Sally is a dumb duck
A little grumpy ball of fluff
L ittle but as messy as a racoon
L ove my little dumb ball of fluff
Y ou won't want this sassy, fluffy duck.

Emma George (10)
Keith Primary School, Keith

Diana And Me

D iana, the dancing dolphin, is as big as a school bus
I t plays around at night-time, it dances around with glee. It will always be just Diana and me
A dolphin, can you imagine eating strawberries, munching on everything you may give her?
N ever being nasty, always kind to everyone
A n extraordinary dolphin as you can see, but it will always just be Diana and me.

Lewis Simmers (10)
Keith Primary School, Keith

Perfect Puppy

P eculiar
E nergised after rest
R ough when playing with toys
F ull of joy
E xtraordinary when sleeping
C ute in pictures and clever
T iny, she is a puppy

P oppy is the name
U nder the duvet in bed
P opcorn is its favourite food
P ickles, she hates them
Y o-yos she plays with.

Megan Jamieson (9)
Keith Primary School, Keith

Gold George

G old George is magic, he turns stuff to gold
O ld but loyal
L earning is his favourite thing
D inner is his favourite time

G eorge is adorable and furry
E ngage with him, he's fun and gentle
O bsessed with kindness
R uns up to five miles per hour
G eorge is agile and tame
E xtraordinary he is.

John Young (9)
Keith Primary School, Keith

My Pet, Moonlight

- **M** oonlight has butterfly wings
- **O** h, a fish tail, a wolf head
- **O** h, devil horns and a snake tongue
- **N** ight has some, she flies away in a flash
- **L** ow and high, how she flies
- **I** think she's here, there she is
- **G** o, go, go, let's have fun
- **H** uh?
- **T** en, nine eight, seven, six, five, four, three, two, one, lift-off!

Ellie-Mai Simpson (9)
Keith Primary School, Keith

Dino Human

Dino Human sure is strange
His appearance he can change

His dino teeth are huge and scary
His human legs are long and hairy

I keep him in the shed at night
If he gets out, he gives folk a fright

Around his neck, I put a collar
Only cost around a dollar

Dino Humans are good pets
Just watch out cos he eats vets.

Kaiden Moir (9)
Keith Primary School, Keith

The Hamdog

I have a lovely hamdog, half-hamster, half-hound
He likes to bark and make a lot of sound
His name is Nibbles and he has long claws
He also has really dirty paws
He's really furry, cute and loud
He likes to be messy and laugh
He's tiny, wild and colourful
Every day, he likes to eat
He eats meat and leaves
And then goes to sleep.

Amy Spence (10)
Keith Primary School, Keith

Sassy Sally

S assy Sally is very dangerous
A nd she is clever too
S he can also fly high
S caling up high buildings
Y odelling as she goes

S oft, furry cape flapping in the wind
A lways solving crimes
L earning is her favourite
L eaping through the air
Y ou could never outrun her.

Khianna Mackie (10)
Keith Primary School, Keith

Bulbtle

B ulbtle is a plant turtle with plants on its shell
U p it hops, it can jump so high with a bell
L ettuce is its favourite food
B eing rude is not what he likes
T his species hates violence and fights
L ike dogs, Bulbtle makes a barking noise
E ven though it is rare, it plays with toys.

Brett Barr (10)
Keith Primary School, Keith

Cadanie

C adanie is as cute as a lamb
A t the age of nine, Cadanie is very adventurous
D o you know that Cadanie is very lazy?
A t midnight, Cadanie is very messy
N ews about Cadanie is adorable
I n the day, Cadanie is very clever
E very time it attracts something.

Evie Morison (9)
Keith Primary School, Keith

Gangsta Geo

Gangsta Geo lives by the bins
To see if he can get any spare tins
They have to be beans, of course

All of his friends moan and groan
The smell stinks of a dirty, old bell
His friends look up to him
As you can tell
After all, they're all friends
And that is how this one ends.

Lauren Sinclair (10)
Keith Primary School, Keith

Magnificent Magna

My dog's name is Magna
She's a big, fluffy lass
She's a superhero
One of the best
She's always up for the test
A special dog she is
She loves her fluffy toys
If you try to take them off her
She will bite
So try not to fight
She's the only one of her kind.

Finlay Marwick (9)
Keith Primary School, Keith

Cabunsnake

C ute as a lamb
A fragile creature
B undle of joy
U nderneath the blanket
N o pickles in her diet
S he is a girl
N o one bothers her in her sleep
A dorable when she is asleep
K ept laughing when I fell
E xtraordinary.

Olivia Bury (9)
Keith Primary School, Keith

Murtle

M y peculiar pet is a mongoose mixed with a turtle
U nder the sea this creature lives
R eally, this pet is simply awesome
T his pet is very cute and funny but very peculiar
L inguine is Murtle's favourite food
E pic is what this pet is and very cool!

Angus Duncan (9)
Keith Primary School, Keith

Lazy Larri

L azy Larri
A sassy snail
Z zzzs and yawns
Y ou might see him flying with his balloons

L ying around
A very lazy snail
R idiculously tiny
R aspberries are his favourite treat
I n the night, he likes to sleep.

Skye Fraser (10)
Keith Primary School, Keith

Jeremy, The Giraffe

Jeremy the giraffe is a very good laugh
He has a pair of roller skates
That make him look daft

Jeremy has big brown patches
He likes to watch football matches

My giraffe has a very long neck
He likes to go on great long treks.

Ryan McWilliam (10)
Keith Primary School, Keith

Tiny Tiger

T wo sizes too small
I ncredible energy
N ice personality
Y ou would like him a lot

T hink he's funny
I s very silly
G oofy laugh
E xtraordinary
R uns very fast.

Edith Malcolm (9)
Keith Primary School, Keith

Rockstar The Racoon

Rockster the racoon
Will come and see you soon
He is super friendly
He is really cool and trendy
Rockster likes to go for a run
He also likes to have fun
Every day he goes to school
Then after, he'll go to the pool.

Callum Duncan (9)
Keith Primary School, Keith

Cuddly Cat

C ute
L oveable
E xtraordinary
V ery naughty
E veryone loves her
R ascal

C uddly
O ver the top
C harming
O bedient.

Meg Malcolm (9)
Keith Primary School, Keith

Dough Ring

Dough Ring is a keyboard playing
Super cool pet
He has himself a vet
He is as agile as a crocodile
He has a car
It's red and shiny
He'll drive it in the night.

Aiden Rodger (9)
Keith Primary School, Keith

Malie The Catfish

Mermaid in the day, cat in the night
A little black cat
Learning his magic so he can fight
I love him, he is the best
Everybody is his best friend.

Lily Ewan (9)
Keith Primary School, Keith

The Grouchy Cat

Humble, heart-warming and honest Father Ash
Despite that, he earns the nickname The Grouchy Cat
If you tell him your untold wish
He will keep it safe like he keeps his mice stew in his dish

His fur is a luscious chocolatey caramel in colour
More like a raw honeycomb
Although sadly, it wasn't meant to taste
A kitten was once deceived
And dared to have a lick
And what came out wasn't as sweet
But a part of his fleece

His eyes were a sapphire blue
And if you peered into them
You would be able to visualise
A scene of all types of birds
Swooping and flipping in the air
Like swallows, eagles and finches

There was a day in particular
The day Father Ash gave a small smile
And I have no intention of forgetting that
When he walked down the aisle
And yes, not only is he moody, mad and miffed
But he also puts on a whiff of priest's perfect powder
So his voice can project louder
The usual mass skippers, but on Easter day
Hurled their beloved kittens
Occupying the front benches
Only to spend the hour religiously
Praying for the speech to end
And the egg hunt to trend
But even though the kittens
Were eager to start the hunt in time
They surprisingly enjoyed his plenary
The most from this prime

For now, the mass has ended
The kittens sidled up to Father Ash
Exclaiming,
"Thank you, Father Ash!"

And that's how a bunch of
Irresistible naughty, noisy, yet cute, kittens
Changed the grouchy cat's mood
What a priest's pet!

Noora Al-Bazi (11)
St Gregory's RC Primary School, Ealing

The Bearbczdw Funny Word Poem

B stands for bizarre pets that dress weirdly and go crazy like a wavy.
E stands for energetic, that means that pets run around like a monkey to have fun.
A stands for amazing pets that are as pretty as a human, you truly are coolly.
R stands for a refreshing drink with a crazy elephant and a wavy giraffe.
B stands for going on a bus but no one is driving except some mice and a little quiet mice house.
C stands for going to the circus and seeing a bunch of animals doing peculiar stuff and doing schooler things.
Z stands for zoology when you go to the museum about zoology, the animals are just screaming and beaming with joy.
D stands for dog but not just an ordinary dog, a magic and enchanted dog.
W stands for a wacky lion that can't stop moving and touching children.

Julia Cheesman (8)
St Gregory's RC Primary School, Ealing

Montgomery, The Marvellous Mole

My peculiar pet's name is Montgomery, who's a marvellous mole
And he is millions of times more clever than the average soul
His amazing capabilities will unquestionably impress
And he uses his startling powers to the excess.

This fantastic beast is the world's wisest creature
And anyone would be honoured to have him as their teacher
His intelligence and brilliance is beyond measure
And his knowledge and perception is a great treasure.

This unique animal's astonishing gadgets are very useful
And many people find their powerful functions very fruitful
They can protect the user from danger in a perilous position
And making more awesome instruments is his ambition!

A critter with superb mathematical skills is very rare
And solving complex algebraic problems is undoubtedly his flair
The pace he solves numerical equations at is outstanding
And lots of people say his sophistication is still expanding!

The source of this bizarre mammal's powers remains very weird
However, his extraordinary talents are not to be feared
Because of his helpful skills, there isn't a single person who's smarter
And all these fabulous abilities are just for starters!

Dominik Kaim (11)
St Gregory's RC Primary School, Ealing

My Pretty Cat Joe

The fortnight ago, I acquired a cat,
He was very nice and embracing and black like a blackboard.
I don't understand why no lovers of cats purchased him,
I was blessed when I saw his eyes, my heart beat fast.
But what the market had forgotten to tell,
Is that this cat is unique in his envious way,
Because every night when the sun goes down,
He sits up tall and begins to miaow.
Oh dear, I thought, *he's a wild cat - tiger black,*
But true fact is, and I'm not making this up.
In the darkness of every night,
He grows thick hairs around his neck and takes off into the dark,
Around the backyard and into the neighbour's.
He zooms through the streets like a police officer.
He's a big cat among cats
Now also strong and conscious too.
I realised what I could do,

As his tiger nature appeared,
I showed him more love.
Off he went, up into the high streets.
Before I realised it!
We strolled, through parks and streets, hands waving and delighted I was.
So now whenever the darkness of the night comes,
Me and my cat walk through the streets like police officers on duty.
A peculiar pet, this cat with tiger looks,
But to me, he is lovely, the most pretty cat.

David George
St Gregory's RC Primary School, Ealing

My Moonlight Owl

Through my eyes
I glimpse at a mythical owl
That can growl
Luna is its name
It is black like the colourless, inky sky
Its eyes are made of leaves
It smells just like lavender
The moon smiles as it flies
Some of its delicate feathers
Glow bright white like the stars

But don't underestimate it
For it's the protector of the night
You're lucky if you catch a glimpse of its shadow
It can fly through memories
To bring back a precious memory
When you look into its large eyes
Memories will fly into your head

It has no fear
For confidence and bravery is in its blood

It can fly to space
To see its moon ancestors
It can breathe underwater
To find a priceless treasure
It can become invisible
To solve frightening crimes
It can even do the impossible

It is still alive today
So if you find an owl
With jet-black feathers
And envious green eyes
Just know that you are
The luckiest person in the world.

Rihanna Sriskantharajah (10)
St Gregory's RC Primary School, Ealing

Dangerous Dylan

He's stealthy, he's nimble, he's crafty, he's agile
He's also a pet hamster and though he's only in his teens
He's simply not as sweet and soft as he really seems
He wears a little bowler hat perched upon his head
And a black bow tie he wears, even in his bed
He sneaks around the house at night upon his silent paws
Down the stairs and through the corridor
Under countless locked up doors
He seeks the cook, who once took his precious smelly cheese
His one possession, to his frustration, his owners hated more than fleas
He snuck into cook's crowded bedroom, it really was a tip
He bared his teeth and turned cook into a hamster with one nip
The next morning, bright and early
The story's blaring on the news
Of the cook who once took Dylan's precious smelly cheese

Yet despite his revenge on that poor, poor person
Dylan knows what he wants to be
He'll take over the world someday, just you wait and see.

Aimee Paget (11)
St Gregory's RC Primary School, Ealing

Lucky's Story

Once, I strode through a park,
The flowerbeds a riot of colour.
My gentle dog Lucky, let out a gleeful bark.
And the park just couldn't be fuller.

I ran for the green gates,
Lucky ran ahead before I could say, "Stay!"
I heard a car hit the brakes,
Silence, then she began to drift away.

I rushed into the vets, Lucky in my arms.
They worked on her for hours on end,
I wish I could take back her harms.
Anything I would fix, I would mend.

When she came out, I thought I would cry.
I ran over to stroke her soft fur,
I saw her bionic side, there was nothing to hide.
But now the past is a distant blur.

Now I stride through the park,
The flowerbeds still a riot of colour.

My half bionic dog lets out a gleeful bark
And my heart couldn't be fuller.

Thomas Jeffs (11)
St Gregory's RC Primary School, Ealing

DJ Shark

DJ shark had dangerous jaws
Which scared the other fish
When they were on the dance floor
His smile was as white as the clouds in the sky
And his teeth twinkled brightly to the beats
As did the lights.

As the music played longer, his fin got larger
And it swooshed right behind him for all to see
He became gigantic and ferocious
As the disco went on
And the sea creatures began to shiver.

The next song came on, that all the fish loved
They all knew the actions and moves
DJ Shark looked excited and turned up the sound
It was time for the party groove.

As the clownfish boogied
He bumped into Dori
They giggled and jiggled with delight
The seahorses bobbed to the musical beat
And the crowd sang loudly to this... 'baby shark'.

Eva McLoughlin (9)
St Gregory's RC Primary School, Ealing

The Story Of A Nurtle

A little turtle, all miniature and delightful
Every day his confidence gets blown away
Three bullies at school mock him
Saying he looks like such a fool
Even though he tries his hardest to be cool.

He hid in his lairy but delightful shell
Feeling lonely, he said to himself,
"I'm such an outcast
Why do I have to be this way?
I need to get this ugliness out of my way!"

One day, he came up with a solution
That eating more could be a revolution
All the fat could burn the colourfulness away
So he ate and ate but the colours didn't go away.

In the end, the shell became even more colourful and neon
The bullies and everyone loved him
He looked wonderful and that's a great tale.

Connor Devlin (11)
St Gregory's RC Primary School, Ealing

Mixed Pet And A Wild, Extraordinary One

My peculiar pet is awesome
It comes from the ocean
It has a mermaid tail and an old, rusty turtle shell
The mermaid tail shimmers like the ocean
And if you want to know then I shall tell you
It has a neon shark fin
It has huge, orange, scaly tentacles
And outside those tentacles it has black skin from the octopus
Those tentacles have furry but smooth bumps
It has an amazing long scorpion tail
Giraffe spots and zebra stripes too
A dino head and the wings glitter when he flies
It also has a cat tail
It has little spikes
It looks like an alien
It is a peculiar pet with abilities
It can fly, breathe fire and ice
It can breathe underwater

It can also change its size and shape
It can change to whatever.

Kacper Sporek (9)
St Gregory's RC Primary School, Ealing

Flo, The Flying Fox

Flo, the flying fox
Oh, how ferocious she is
She only comes out at night
But only when it's not bright

Flo is a fox
Who is never really bored
She sleeps in a box
Which is made of cardboard

She only comes out at night
Because of her extraordinary powers
She doesn't think it's right
For anyone to see her when there is light

But only I have seen her
In my garden, she flies beyond the stars
But my mum didn't believe me
While she was sorting out the food jars

Oh, she never believes me
I thought to myself

If only I could sneak out
Behind the tree after tea
And call her in
Unless she is deaf, of course.

Flossie O'Meara (11)
St Gregory's RC Primary School, Ealing

Baldy, My Cat

Look at my bald cat
She looks like she is inside out
She has no fur and she is always cold
That's how it is when you are bald!

Best friend that always hides under your duvet
And when you tell her to go away she gets upset!
She wakes me up every morning
With one big yawning.

I have to admit her breath smells so bad
But she refused when I offered her Tic-Tac.
She is so small and looks so cute
But when we take her jumpers off she has an attitude.

My other two cats at first were so confused
They looked at her, they looked at each other and were so amused!
Is it a rat? Why is this cat inside out?
Oh! It's just a Sphinx cat
That's why she is inside out!

No matter if you have fur or not
They love each other and run together like they lost the plot!

Lucas A (8)
St Gregory's RC Primary School, Ealing

Pando, The Panda

Pando the panda roams around
Looking at everything he can see
The sea speaks, trees talk in a peculiar sound
But Pando isn't an ordinary panda, you'll see
Pando walked to Germany
"Hallo!"
He went to Spain
"Holaa!"
The wild, colourful creature roamed in Paris
"Bonjour!"
Yes, you see, Pando speaks lots of languages
Pando the panda pops to places
Jumping excitedly, talking as if he's wearing braces
But other animals are inspired by him
Talking and hoping they spoke like him
Pando is perfect
Pando is great
As all the other animals are too.

Olivia Miller-Noya (11)
St Gregory's RC Primary School, Ealing

George, The Gaming Puppy

George is my puppy, he is very cute
When we play video games he gets the best loot
He has blonde hair and is really fluffy
Leaving treat wrappers on the floor, he's so scruffy
Every now and then, he needs a scrubby
With the amount of food he eats, he is quite chubby
Morning and evening, we will go on a walk
In reality, I wish he could talk
Wearing his headset
To us, no one is a titanic of a threat
He likes to think he's extremely cool
In the game, he will make people look like a fool
This poem is for George, my best buddy
Remember, when you go on walks, don't get your dog muddy!

Dante Kulasingam (10)
St Gregory's RC Primary School, Ealing

Seamouse

This little sea mouse likes to bite
He's half-shark and half-mice
This little mouse swims in his blouse
He sleeps with it too
In his cosy boathouse
The mouse eats with it too
But he only eats sprouts
Sprouts are his favourite
But special cause they're sea sprouts
He's only called a seamouse
Because he likes the sea
He's under the sea
Because he disagrees with fleas
Fleas are so itchy
They've got to show mercy
We've got to waste our time drinking tea
Because you little fleas don't understand the plea
So now under the sea, the seamouse is free!

Sara Iwaniec
St Gregory's RC Primary School, Ealing

Jellyog And I

Jellyog is a jelly-made hog,
With eyes that can see for miles.
First I found him stuck in a bog,
Surrounded by crocodiles.

I jumped on his back and headed home,
Where we knew we'd be safe.
He stays in my room asleep by a trough,
And eats so much food, he's no waif!

We went on a journey to the city,
Flew so high our toes almost froze,
While we were there, we met Professor Chris Witty.
Fun fact: A lot about COVID he knows.

Once returned home, he said he must leave.
"Why?" I cried and hugged him tightly.
"There is a friend in the bog I need to retrieve,"
He turned and trotted off lightly.

Edward Jeffs (9)
St Gregory's RC Primary School, Ealing

Manticore Bill

My pet is called Manticore Bill, he is a very strange creature.
But what about its features?
A human face, with hair like lace
A lion's body, not too shoddy
And a scorpion's tail, purple and pale
He eats real slow and runs really fast
He likes to play in the snow and eat lots of grass
Yes! Bill has his fill of rose bushes and daffodils
With every move he makes, his tail follows like a snake
It's not poisonous, full of kindness and joyfulness
Bill loves to dance and make noise with us
I love taking care of my Manticore, it never feels like a chore
He's the bestest, most strangest pet in the world
Who can ask for more?

Mykah Perez (9)
St Gregory's RC Primary School, Ealing

My Dinorompus

Left, right, left, right,
Oh what a happy sight,
Walking down the corridor,
Shouting with one big roar!
Crunch, munch, crunch, munch,
Treading down the hall for lunch,
A few peas and a lot of meat,
Enough to run the massive feet,
Run to work and run to play,
For the rest of this monstrous day,
Four long arms and one big head,
Ready to hop on a snowy sled,
Slide down roads and slide down hills,
What a lot of monstrous skills!
Now we got to this guy's home,
A massive bed for a massive bone,
A tiny body,
Four long arms,
Massive feet and massive throne,
A long day deserves some rest,
Finally a comfy bed at its best.

Philip Strzelczyk (9)
St Gregory's RC Primary School, Ealing

Danny, The Bizarre Doggy

Danny, my little doggy
Wasn't like the other ones
He would sit like a human
And play chess with my neighbour's sons

He would walk on two legs
And read and write
He would even hang my coat
On my special wooden pegs

He would attend the weekly book club
And be a book-loving Einstein
And when he would come home
He would recline on a chair in the blazing hot sunshine

Danny, my little doggy
Strongly believed he was a real person
But would be surrounded by melancholy
When we would tell him that he wasn't.

Caroline Sideso (11)
St Gregory's RC Primary School, Ealing

Arthur The Superhero

Arthur the superhero cat sat on a mat
He isn't just any cat
He is a super cat on his special mat
It isn't just any mat, it was a super mat.

He had an enemy called Mr Rat
Who went round the neighbourhood annoying the cats
That's when they sent for help
And in flew Arthur with a scratch and a yelp.

Arthur sharpened his claws to give an almighty scratch
That was the beginning of the end for Mr Rat
Because he was no match.

The superhero had saved the day and all the cats cheered
There was nobody in the world that Arthur the superhero feared.

Myles Pierce (8)
St Gregory's RC Primary School, Ealing

My Unidogzepony

My unidogzepony is a really strange pet
It's a unicorn, dog, zebra and pony all in one
She loves food depending on her mood
Sometimes she is happy and sometimes she is lonely
Whenever she is sad it gets really bad
She loves going to different places in the world
And she thinks hot dogs are babies
And she thinks her name is Hayley
She likes unidogs aka hot dogs
She drinks this unicorn drink every day and says it's a magic potion
She walks in slow motion
She thinks she can fly but she jumps in the air, saying goodbye.

Michaela Kesselly-Moore (9)
St Gregory's RC Primary School, Ealing

My Dino-Lemur

My dino-lemur is sassy and spotty
He's full of freckles on his nose and face
And he wears an eyepatch every day
His cheeks are as red as fire
His jingly clown hat is as colourful as ever
His stripes are multicoloured
His claws are sharp and his paws are large
His ears are shaped like mushrooms
And steam spreads in his ears
He has a moustache as curly as can be
His teeth are as sharp as a sword
His eyes are the shape of ovals
His feet are short like a sausage dog's
My dino-lemur has a little bit of everything.

Giuliana Sofia Franklin Tijaro (8)
St Gregory's RC Primary School, Ealing

Private Investigator Swalk

P rivate Investigator Swalk
E xuberant colourful coat of fur
C unningly, Swalk devised his next move
U tterly abnormal, the reptilian-like Swalk
L urked around
I nvestigating what curious crimes he needs to solve next
A ware of his odour
R eeking from foul water from years spent in the sewers

P rivate Investigator Swalk
E normous snake to tiny worm
T irelessly patrolling streets by day
S lithering silently in the sewers by night.

Khloe Francis Nwaka (10)
St Gregory's RC Primary School, Ealing

Bella

When I take my dog for a walk
He's scared of a noisy talk
People running, children shouting
He is hiding behind a rock

Come on, look, Bella
Bumblebees buzzing in the bluebells
The dormouse darted past
But he is running fast

Has he never seen a cat?
Has he never heard a bat?
Has he never seen a house?
Has he never chased a mouse?

What a peculiar puppy, I think
This lockdown has made him shrink
Be brave, bark, chase
But all he does is hide in the maze.

Julia Trzeciak (11)
St Gregory's RC Primary School, Ealing

Constable Clive Chameleon

Constable Clive Chameleon
Was held in great esteem
By the village that he lived in
And his loyal crime-fighting team
He caught so many criminals
Using vision, smell and sound
It is also very helpful
That he could blend into the background
Sometimes he wears a uniform
That is blue, pink or grey
It depends on what kind of mood he's in
But it changes colour every day
One time, he ate a pencil
And we took him to the vet
So I had to miss playing cops and robbers
With my peculiar pet.

Layla Keenan (11)
St Gregory's RC Primary School, Ealing

The Markiosaurus

There once was a mysterious creature,
He had more than one bizarre feature.
Some called him a monster at first sight,
But in practice, he was actually quite bright.
His arms were scaly and long,
But do not underestimate how strong.
His legs were slim and short,
But more than enough to support.
His hands were oddly round,
With razor-sharp claws that did surround,
Altogether he was entirely brown.
The most odd thing about him was his head,
Triangular and aerodynamic, but do not be misled.
Half human, half dinosaur,
His name was Markiosaurus.

Hugo Pawlak
St Gregory's RC Primary School, Ealing

The 200-Foot Beetle

I once had an encounter
With a 200-foot beetle
It is one of the most dreadful creatures
You will ever come across.

Its eyes are scarlet red
Its body is pitch-black
And is as strong as Godzilla.

Its appetite is usually
300 or 400 humans a day.

In one single punch
It could smash The Shard easily.

It's as deadly as 100 elephants
Orcas, snakes and lions combined.

It's very endangered
So, there's not much to worry about
Just keep alert, just in case you happen to meet one.

Giacomo Collins (8)
St Gregory's RC Primary School, Ealing

My Snake, Blake

I have an unusual pet snake.
His name is Blake.
He likes to gobble up delicious cake.
He eats it at an extraordinary rate.
Wow, isn't that great!
He's my soulmate.
Although we always hang out,
He's a mate I'd like to learn more about.
He'll always come to my side when he hears my shout.
Curled and snuggled up in his glass tank.
Where he unwinds after he sank.
He's my number-one rank.
And I've got him to thank.
I love my emerald snake dearly.
You can see that very clearly.
And we go out and about together yearly.

Sebastian Grundy (8)
St Gregory's RC Primary School, Ealing

Animalsaurus Rex!

A nimalsaurus Rex!
N othing is more peculiar than this!
I t ate half the moon last week,
M y brain can't digest this!
A world of oddness awaits me,
"L et me eat Mars, I've heard It's chocolatey!" he whines,
"S o what?" I reply absentmindedly,
A nimalsaurus Rex!
U h-oh... He's destroyed the front lawn!
R exy's not that well-behaved if I was to be honest...
U gh, what's he done now?
S o why did I adopt him?

Francesca Studnik (9)
St Gregory's RC Primary School, Ealing

Bond Bono

Bond Bono is a secret spy
He can't be spotted with the naked human eye
He walks up the stairs, not petrified
He's so courageous he never cried
Bono's white like a daisy flake
He's more menacing than a venomous snake
He's cleaner than a new bubbly bath
Nothing could ever disturb his path
His vapid, swollen eyes are never fasten
Until his target starts to hasten
He is a dog that is extremely brisk
That if you run, you're taking a major risk.

Michal Brogowski (10)
St Gregory's RC Primary School, Ealing

Marcus, The Marvellous Mathmat

Marcus is a peculiar pet
He is hardly a threat
But when you challenge him to a quiz
He will defeat you in a whizz
He is also extremely lazy
If you don't do what he says
He will make you go crazy

Marcus is a child of seven
The place was anything but heaven
He was the smartest cat in the group
His favourite food is a bowl of pea soup
So if you approach him with his tail up high
Remember, never ever call yourself a wise guy.

Melissa Griffin (11)
St Gregory's RC Primary School, Ealing

Sid The Snake Dragon

Sid the snake dragon hunts for food,
The animals in the cave run for cover when he's in this mood!
He lives in the dark with a bear and a dog,
And they often fight about who gets to sit on the log!
Sid's scales often give children a fright,
And they run away with all their might
When they see him slither and slide through the grass
All they are trying to do is get to class!
Sid loves his music
He likes to listen to rock
Sometimes he plays it so loud he gives humans a shock!

Alexander Owsiany
St Gregory's RC Primary School, Ealing

Maximus Fish

Maximus is a peculiar fish
Who would not drink from the dish
While I munch my lunch
Maximus has his bubble punch
When I see lots of bubbles
Maximus has lots of troubles
He is hiding among the rocks
I know he laughs and mocks
He is friends with my lobster
Who is really a big mopster
Together, they terrorise little shrimps
That tremble and one of them even limps
My aquarium has a gang
That it's quiet when I bang.

Alan Nerka (10)
St Gregory's RC Primary School, Ealing

Blazey The Bear

B lazey is a little cub
L emons are his favourite grub
A cardboard box is his treasured lair
Z illions of things he keeps in there
E asy does it, don't wake him up
Y ou're in a pickle, you dropped a cup!

B rown, soft, snuggly warm
E ven though his fur's like a storm
A beautiful bear, so tiny and clever
R hyming this poem for him was no problem whatsoever!

Patryk Tober (11)
St Gregory's RC Primary School, Ealing

Bert, The Bank-Robbing Bunny

Have you ever heard of the bank-robbing bunny?
Eyes red like a tomato, fur grey like a thundercloud,
Claws as sharp as a T-rex's tooth and a squeak so loud.
When you see this creature, you'd better run!

While you're on your trip to the shops,
You may see this bunny driving along the road,
But don't worry, it'll be on a mobility scooter, eating a toad,
So you better watch out, NatWest, because it's coming your way!

Adam Chorebala (11)
St Gregory's RC Primary School, Ealing

My Terrible Turtle, Tubbo

My turtle, Tubbo, can do almost anything
He can run, he can have fun
But most importantly, he can get the job done
Send him to deliver your package
He'll get it done without any damage

Because Tubbo is a super turtle
He can run, he can have fun
He'll be your best friend
To the very, very end

My turtle, Tubbo, can do almost anything
He loves to run and have fun
My terrific turtle, Tubbo, is the best.

Ruslana Balabukh (11)
St Gregory's RC Primary School, Ealing

Peperami, My Favourite Cat

My favourite cat is called Peperami

He's a bit of an animal
He loves to lie in the scorching summer sun
He's long and thin, tied up with string
He sizzles on the big brick barbecue
His body is twice the size of my other cats
He loves to relax in the frying pan or a hot dog bun
His paws are way too small for his long body
He covers himself in brown sauce and mustard

That's because he's a sausage cat!

Orla Fryatt (10)
St Gregory's RC Primary School, Ealing

My Dream Pet

Once, I had an incredible dog called Pog
He was extremely cute
Pog wasn't that good at tricks
Yet he always seemed to surprise me
He took me to school in the most bizarre ways
On Monday by a plane
On Tuesday by a helicopter
On Wednesday by a car
On Thursday by a hot air balloon
On Friday, for some reason, by a shopping trolley
I smiled to myself as I was woken up by my alarm
That really was my dream pet.

Mateusz Szarek (11)
St Gregory's RC Primary School, Ealing

Lotus' Big Day

One day Little Lotus was walking down the streets
Whilst munching on some sweets
Some people nicknamed her Kattycorn
Because she was a cat crossed with a unicorn
She treated herself to dinner
Because it was getting dimmer
All of these goodies in one day
As it was her birthday on Friday
When she went to sleep
Her dreams got really deep
She dreamed of having friends
Because her story never ends.

Olivia Fashade (9)
St Gregory's RC Primary School, Ealing

Night And Day

My catdragacorn called Rainbow
Is as mischievous as a monkey
And as cute as koala
In the day, it is cute and gentle.
It has all the colours of the rainbow
Its horn is shiny and gold
Its eyes are adorable and sparkly
When night comes
It turns into an evil monster
With black on its back
Teeth sticking out
And its horn twisted all up
And eyes all white
Wings spiked up
The end!

Emma Lukomska (9)
St Gregory's RC Primary School, Ealing

Waffle

I have a pet gorilla,
He is a banana tree killer,
His name is Waffle and he is such a thriller,
And he keeps a secret food stash in the chiller,
Waffle walks down to town,
And acts like a clown,
While the shop owners have a frown,
As we buy all their food,
At noon our fridge would burst,
And Mum would have no money in her purse,
And Dad would say, "This is a curse!"
At 10 o'clock Waffle would be in bed, needing a nurse!

Tala Glover (9)
St Gregory's RC Primary School, Ealing

Tom, The Terrific Turtle

He's adorable
He's incredible
He's cute
He's tiny

But he has a dark side
And he never likes to hide
You can't see him coming
You can't tell when he is running

When he's running
He is as slow as the sun
Moving around the Earth
He never wants help
But he knew how everyone felt
He was a dangerous turtle
But everyone liked him.

Anaiya Rainford-Celestine (11)
St Gregory's RC Primary School, Ealing

My Peculiar Pet Fish!

My peculiar fish is the greatest fish.
It must feel good to swim for a while.
The tank is a mystery.
It's calling and alerting me.
A beam of light shines in his fish tank
To see the world on show
He starts dancing and showing his dance moves.
His friend joins and starts showing off his curls and twirls.
He is my peculiar pet because he's great at dancing
Even though he is peculiar, he is a little fish and I love him.

Amelia Wright (9)
St Gregory's RC Primary School, Ealing

Super Dog

Super Dog saves the city every day
If you asked him about it, he wouldn't say
He saves cats from lamp posts, Squirrels from bins
Granny's handbags and robbers from their sins.
Super Dog saves the city every day
He makes sure the bad people never get away!
He gets the kids to school, the traffic to flow
If you see a problem, be sure to let him know!
Super Dog saves my city every day!
And I love him in every single way!

Arlo Johnstone (9)
St Gregory's RC Primary School, Ealing

Pikado's Day

One day Pikado went to the garden,
He jumped in the pool and played with his favourite ball.
He walked to the park and met his friend
They played and played
The fun didn't end
Pikado walked home
He went inside and saw the snow and ran outside.
He made a snowman, it came alive
It was the best day of his life.
When the snow stopped he was very sad,
He had dinner, he was happy and glad.

Shannon Moynihan (9)
St Gregory's RC Primary School, Ealing

Mrs Girraficorn

I took my Girraficorn out on a walk,
We walked for 20 minutes and then Mrs Girraficorn's horn lit up.
Whoosh!
We went in the air!
Wroom!
We flew about 30 minutes
And then down we went.
We fell on top of a tree.
Mrs Girraficorn and I stayed on the tree.
We hung there for about 20 minutes then cleaned up.
Time to go back home!
Vroom!
10 minutes later we got back home.

Luiza Tarasek (9)
St Gregory's RC Primary School, Ealing

Brownie The Bunny

Browine the bunny is cute
But she is sassy, as wild as a lion
But tiny as a puppy
Happy to go out on walks
Carrots are her favourite treat
While whaching TV
But when night comes
She's a superhero in disguise
Keeping the world nice and safe
From bad guys and burglars
Brownie the bunny
Is as furry as a cat
Welcome my pet
Miss Brownie the bunny!

Zaria Fa Kusi
St Gregory's RC Primary School, Ealing

I Saw A Super Hot Sausage Dog

I heard a big bang
Coming from my bedroom
I thought it was a rat
I peeked into my bedroom
There was nothing there
But there was a lot of mess
I suddenly knew
It was something very big
Now I think it is a peculiar pet
It could be a cat saving the day
Or maybe a dog that likes to dance
At the corner of my eye
I saw a sausage dog
It was a super hot sausage dog!

Vivienne Yassa (8)
St Gregory's RC Primary School, Ealing

I Want A Dog But Not Just Any Dog...

I really want a dog
Loo-Lu, she will be named
She will be potty-trained
As lazy as she will be
She will always come on a jog with me.

Adorable and fluffy
She will be a Nutella brown
I will always hold her and never put her down
Although she will be as gentle as a bunny
She will also be ferocious when she finds it funny.

Aoife Stewart (11)
St Gregory's RC Primary School, Ealing

The Superhero Frog

He is green like emeralds
And as slimy as slime
With an IQ of 700
He is good at solving crimes

Hopping from city to city
Catching all the crooks
Helping the police
To solve the crimes on their books

You should never underestimate
The Superhero Frog
He has so many powers
Which makes him the top dog.

Conor Whyte (11)
St Gregory's RC Primary School, Ealing

Doug The Pug

Doug the pug is a hip-hop dog.
He dances and prances
He hops and flops
He glides and slides
He twirls and curls
He shakes and quakes
He loves to been seen
Because he is a machine
When he is done and had his fun
He will wait another day to do it all again
Because he is Doug the pug
The dog who can do hip-hop!

Estella Thompson Oakley (9)
St Gregory's RC Primary School, Ealing

Foxter

- **F** oxter is very dangerous, he has long sharp claws
- **O** nly he can break a brick wall. He can climb anything
- **X** aubab, in North America, he works at a circus
- **T** he circus is in America and he works for it
- **E** very day he enjoys it
- **R** ather than sitting in his den, that's why he works in the circus.

Tymon Urbanowicz (9)
St Gregory's RC Primary School, Ealing

Peculiar Snake

There is a snake
That shoots spiders out of its butt
It has laser eyes
It slithers around most of the time
It kills its prey and eats it for lunch
Its eyes are flaming when it comes to killing
'Cause it kills it, eats it and loves it
Its name is Spider Laser 'cause it's cool
And it is my only pet.

Aaliyah Humphries-Brown (8)
St Gregory's RC Primary School, Ealing

Gilda The Griffin

G riffins are mean but mine is always keen
I deally I would like her to learn a new trick every week
L ovely Gilda is so sweet, Gilda is a griffin you'll want to meet
D angerous but kind, caring but fierce. Brave because she has had her ears pierced
A gile, quick and can do a backflip.

Lily Hunter (9)
St Gregory's RC Primary School, Ealing

Flamindog

F lames come out of his mouth
L azy is his attitude
A ll yellow and black is his beak
M agnificent is the pink of his skin
I nfinite is his neck
N ature is where he lives
D og food he eats
O ften he barks
G entle is his walk.

Tiphaine Riou (11)
St Gregory's RC Primary School, Ealing

Cadolepi

A print like a leopard,
Never seen by a shepherd,
Ears like a kitten,
Can even hear when you sew a mitten,
Body like a puppy,
He loves when you rub his tummy,
Nose like a pig,
Can smell the tiniest stink,
Can do a flying cartwheel into the sky,
And fly up high and see a butterfly.

Olivia Ryan (9)
St Gregory's RC Primary School, Ealing

Spider Dog

Sneaking through the grass
With eight legs, quiet as a mouse
It's as fierce and huge as a giant wild dog
But as venomous as a spider
Its fangs are skyscrapers
Fur as black as coal
It eats raw meat, flies and bugs
As scary as a spider, as fast as a dog!

Adam Holland (11)
St Gregory's RC Primary School, Ealing

My Dog Is A Superhero!

My dog is a superhero,
He defeated Emperor Nero,
He travels at night,
And has a big fight,
And tries to be like a nun,
Then sleeps all day in the sun,
Because my dog is a superhero,
He wears a blue mask,
And a trailing red cape,
And hates Professor Snape,
Because my dog is a superhero!

Elsie May Lettis (9)
St Gregory's RC Primary School, Ealing

Bruno

Fluffy, friendly, cute and nice
Even wild sometimes
Little eyes that blink and blink
Little ears as soft as silk
He cannot sit and be ignored
Sometimes crazy, sometimes lazy
But you can never be bored with him
And that's my pet
Bruno.

Patryk Kozlowski (10)
St Gregory's RC Primary School, Ealing

Dancing Dogs

My dancing dog loves to dance
She can't stop once she starts
She does ballet and tango
But if there was nobody to dance with
She would dance with me
Then she shakes me round the room
Until she let's go
Then I crash and *boom!*

Maria Grazia Della Gatta (9)
St Gregory's RC Primary School, Ealing

The Dogosaur

Stomp! Stomp!
In the background you can see the mighty Dogosaur
He comes with a smash on the building
Chop, chop
He will chop your house
He will laser eye the buildings to the ground
He is the first dogosaur in the world.

Alan Romanczuk
St Gregory's RC Primary School, Ealing

Dancing Dog

My dog loves to dance. Every time she starts she just cannot stop.
She loves to twirl around and she pounces all about.
The only time she stops is when I show her the clock.
Then she goes to bed because it's 8 o'clock.

Saiyen Pillay-Gomes (9)
St Gregory's RC Primary School, Ealing

Alpaca

A mazing animal who drives a sports car
L ikeable by everyone
P ink and unique
A n alpaca named Wilbur
C ute and fluffy like a cloud
A nimal that is one of a kind.

Alex Sobiczewski (10)
St Gregory's RC Primary School, Ealing

My Pet Claws

C an you meet my pet claws?
L ong tail and big claws.
A nd zooms across the room.
W hen I play with her,
S he is a satisfying peculiar pet to know.

Rita Kozub
St Gregory's RC Primary School, Ealing

Alfis Racer!

A mazing acrobatics
L oving talents
F ast Lamborghini
I ncredible car mechanics
S ensational abomination

R ebellious racer!

Tymon Kowalik (9)
St Gregory's RC Primary School, Ealing

The Poem About Justin The Gamer

Justin the gamer, so good at gaming,
Making a cake,
Then eating it off a plate
Justin the gamer, so smart and so strong
Marking his maths paper
Which seems very long.

Excel Etteh (9)
St Gregory's RC Primary School, Ealing

Beautiful Owl

Owl, owl flying in the sky
Owl, owl doing front flips
Owl, owl spinning in the wind
Owl, owl, owl.

Abiana Alexandru (8)
St Gregory's RC Primary School, Ealing

Turtle Fire Monster

T errible and mysterious
U nbelievably scary
R umble in his tummy
T roublesome
L ovely and kind
E xtra intelligent

F earsome and creepy
I ndependent and cool
R ock monster
E legant

M ad cool
O n top of the rock
N ever bad
S cary
T errible at sleeping
E very day, he breathes fire
R ock and roll!

Ava Barr (9)
Woodlands Primary School, Linwood

Robo Rock Alien

R obo Rock Alien likes to rock
O h, he is lazy but incredible
B rilliant and agile
O n his way to Mars

R ocks can never defeat him
O ranges are his favourite
C an drive a UFO
K ing of space

A nd he is also wild
L ol! He's smart at jokes
I ncredible dance moves
E xtraordinary guitar skills
N o way! He is massive!

Jack Irvine (8)
Woodlands Primary School, Linwood

Roboshark

R oboshark is a good pet
O bviously, he is a good pet
B ut he is a bit rough
O range is his favourite colour
S harks are apex predators
H e is super smart
A s rough as he is, he is respectful
R oboshark rules the sea
K rany, his best friend, is good at shark ball, but Roboshark always beats him.

Nathan Kay (9)
Woodlands Primary School, Linwood

Unibubbles

U nafraid of anything
N oisy most of the time
I nspiring at blowing bubbles
B eautiful at art
U nfortunate sometimes
B eautiful at playing the piano
B rilliant at writing poems
L oves cheering and dancing
E xtraordinary at singing
S he is sassy and smart.

Isla Hampsay (8)
Woodlands Primary School, Linwood

Bunnare

B rilliant at drawing
U nique as ever
N ice to people and animals
N aughty sometimes in the kitchen
A bit annoying
R eally kind all the time
E veryone loves her so much.

Hannah Madden (8)
Woodlands Primary School, Linwood

The Lagon

- **L** east known animal on the planet
- **A** lways agile and amazing animal
- **G** rumpy and gigantic
- **O** n the road to be the strongest animal in the world
- **N** ever gonna lose a fight.

Jacob Sindhar (9)
Woodlands Primary School, Linwood

Duck Dog

D uck Dog can fly, he is
U nique and funny, he is
C ute and crazy and
K ind

D ifferent
O range is his favourite colour
G ood at flying.

Kaylah Boyce (9)
Woodlands Primary School, Linwood

Rockstar Rabbit

R ebel songs
O ranges are his favourite food
C ooking is his hobby
K ing of music

O n the road to victory
N ice people are her favourite people.

Laura Reid (8)
Woodlands Primary School, Linwood

Shadow

S hadow is evil
H ops her way to evil
A rgh! Shadow is coming
D ark and evil magic
O h no! Dark magic
W ow! The dark is evil.

James Tweedy (8)
Woodlands Primary School, Linwood

Longe

L ongest bird in the world
O n the World Record
N early zooms along
G iant flying bird
E agles are its worst enemy.

John Ward (9)
Woodlands Primary School, Linwood

Young Writers
Est. 1991

YOUNG wRITERS INFORMATION

We hope you have enjoyed reading this book – and that you will continue to in the coming years.

If you're a young writer who enjoys reading and creative writing, or the parent of an enthusiastic poet or story writer, visit our website www.youngwriters.co.uk/subscribe to join the World of Young Writers and receive news, competitions, writing challenges, tips, articles and giveaways! There is lots to keep budding writers motivated to write!

If you would like to order further copies of this book, or any of our other titles, then please give us a call or order via your online account.

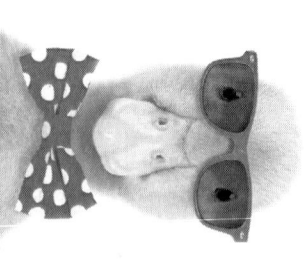

Young Writers
Remus House
Coltsfoot Drive
Peterborough
PE2 9BF
(01733) 890066
info@youngwriters.co.uk

Join in the conversation!
Tips, news, giveaways and much more!

YoungWritersUK YoungWritersCW youngwriterscw